ITTY & BiTTY

Friends on the Farm

written by
Nancy Carpenter Czerw

illustrated by
Rose Mary Berlin

McWITTY PRESS, New York, NY

For Luke and Travis — NCC

To my mother and father, for their love and encouragement. — RMB

Text copyright ©2003 by Nancy Carpenter Czerw
Illustrations copyright ©2006 by Rose Mary Berlin

www.ittyandbitty.com

Book and jacket designed by Kenneth B. Smith

Printed in Hong Kong
First edition
2006

ISBN 0-9755618-3-9

McWITTY PRESS
110 Riverside Dr., 1A
New York, NY 10024

We're Itty and Bitty

From Steele Away Farm-

Two miniature horses

With maximum charm.

We get into mischief,

But never do harm.

When we get close to trouble
Molly barks out Alarm!

We play, trim the grass,

And our barn friends agree-

We're the best mini-mascots
That you'll ever see!

Troy is tall and brown and sleek,

But he's too big for Hide and Seek.

We always win - it's no surprise.

Our smallness is a better size-

To hide in bushes, barn, or garage.

And our spots are perfect camouflage.

Sasha is a Dog of Flanders.

Her proper name is Bouvier.

She longs to herd some calves or cows,
But not these friends who "neigh."

Bitty is a jolly sport,

And a most obliging fellow.

He lets her chase him 'round the pond,
While he tries to "moo" and "bellow."

When dinnertime is on the way,

Big horses stomp and snort and neigh,

Demanding carrots, oats, and hay.

We eat much less, as you might guess,

And think that being polite is best.

To get our share (we're small, not skinny!)

We ask with a little mini-whinny.

Splash and Scrabble

Are tall and fleet.

When they

start running

we dodge their   feet!

Molly and Sasha are more our size,
But we help everyone exercise.

From sunrise to sunset,

The game never ends,

As we race to keep up
With our bigger friends!